For Therese, Julie, Carol, Marty, Peter, Charlie,
Lucy, and Rosemary—berriers all.   E.P.

For the most beautiful berries in my marmalade:
Molly, Samuel, Matthew, and Rubia.   N.C.

Text copyright © 2004 by Ethel Pochocki
Illustrations copyright © 2004 by Normand Chartier
Dust-jacket and interior design by Lindy Gifford
Printed in China

7   6   5   4   3   2   1

ISBN 0-89272-558-3
Library of Congress Control Number 2004105178

Down East Books
P.O. Box 679
Camden, ME 04843
A division of Down East Enterprise, publishers of Down East *magazine, www.downeast.com*

To request a book catalog or place an order, visit www.downeastbooks.com, or call 800-685-7962.

Maine Marmalade

By ETHEL POCHOCKI

Illustrated by NORMAND CHARTIER

Down East Books
Camden, Maine

There once was a boy named Anthony who lived on the coast of Maine. He wanted to do just one special thing. He didn't want to ride in the milk truck at dawn or catch a mackerel by himself or sit on his neighbor's motorcycle and pretend he was riding it through the woods.

What he wanted to do more than anything was make a batch of jam. He had wanted to do this since he first went with his mother to search the boggy fields and shore cliffs and abandoned orchards of Cape Rosier for wild fruit.

On that special day, they left after the breakfast dishes had been washed and the bread had been set to rise. His mother packed a lunch of sandwiches made with Swiss cheese and dill pickles on pumpernickel bread, and put in a thermos of lemonade. Oh, how good this would taste to the weary searchers as they rested beneath an apple tree!

They climbed the hill at the top of the Cape, where the wind blew in from the cove and sang in the leaves of the birches. Here Anthony stood, King of the Hill, atop the ledges where gulls dropped clamshells like pieces of a puzzle.

And here they found patches of wild strawberries or low-lying dewberries or the gleanings left by the blueberry rakers. Past the red cedars, which smelled like ripe peaches, were magnificent blackberry brambles. Even though Anthony wore an old flannel shirt, the prickly vines and canes reached out and grabbed him like the bony fingers of a witch.

But he kept right on picking the berries, purplish black and juicy and large as a thimble—or even his own thumb. (His mother laughed when he later printed THUMBLEBERRY JAM on the jar label.)

Next, Anthony climbed the wild crabapple tree and
shook down a rain of rosy nuggets. He scaled the cliffs with an
old lard bucket tied to his belt and gathered rose hips as big as
apricots. He waded in a stream and picked the elderberries
growing along the bank. And when Anthony and his mother
found gooseberries, he cut off their blossom ends with his
own knife.

When they came home, he helped her hull the fruit and
pick out stems and pits. He measured sugar, often without
spilling it, and put the wax in the old metal teapot to melt.
Anthony thought it was the most exciting thing in the world to
watch his mother fill the jars with jelly that sparkled like rubies.

But that was last year. Now Anthony was older. He didn't want to help his mother; he wanted to do it all himself. He dreamed of entering a jar of incredibly wonderful jam in the Blue Hill Fair and winning first prize. Then he'd go on to be best in Maine—and maybe even in the whole United States!

Anthony shared his dream with no one because he didn't want to be laughed at. He decided that he would pick the fruit first, then he would tell his mother.

Anthony discovered this was easier said than done, for he could not find enough of any one fruit to make even a single jar of jam. It was August, and the strawberries had already gone by. Nor could he find any raspberries. Another seeker must have picked them. The currant and gooseberry bushes bore only a handful of fruit that the birds had left from their breakfast. When he climbed Blueberry Hill, he found the fruit still hard and small and pink, and in the bog, the cranberries that crunched under his feet were still green.

Anthony was disappointed. He went home and moped and sulked, and he would not tell his mother what was wrong. He pushed aside his peanut-butter-and-honey sandwich and kicked the kitchen table leg over and over again. His mother's patience grew thin.

"Anthony, stop spreading gloom and doom around, and make yourself useful. Go out to the garden, please, and get one zucchini, three carrots, a sprig of dill, and some green beans. Just enough for a bowl of vegetables for supper. How do you think that will taste?"

Anthony didn't answer. He just made a face and went to the garden. He didn't *care* how they would taste. But as he picked, a small, wonderful idea stirred in his mind. He hurried the vegetables back to the kitchen, almost smiling in his better mood.

"Well," said his mother, giving him a funny look, "I never knew work to cause such an instant cure. Anthony, stop hopping like that! My cake will fall. I swear you must have fleas!"

The next morning Anthony woke earlier than usual. He dressed in an old shirt with long sleeves, jeans with patched knees, and sneakers with holes in the toes. He ate a bowl of cornflakes with a banana and then set off for a field behind the house. He told himself he would follow any path, wherever it led, and pick whatever fruit he found.

He watched a blue butterfly zigzag its way to a Juneberry tree, where six berries waited in one pink cluster. Into his pail they went. Beneath the tree, two small bushes nudged each other, and Anthony saw the crimson of currants and the green of gooseberries, just a handful. They joined the Juneberries, and soon the bottom of his pail was covered.

He picked his way through the wet grass and found some dewberry vines creeping along the edge of the woods. Their fruit was not as big and fat as thimbleberries but tasted just as sweet. A small patch of early blueberries lay beside the dewberry vine, all ripe and ready to go into his pail, which was now almost one-quarter full.

Anthony hurried from the field to the path that led into
the woods, pretending as he ran that he was a Penobscot Indian
scout being chased by a black bear. Or maybe *he* was chasing
the bear. Anthony hadn't decided which when he came out of
the woods to the shore. Chokecherries hung heavy from the
slim trees that were staggering down the cliff. He jumped up
to catch the branches and held them down with one hand
while he picked cherries with the other. The pail was begin-
ning to feel heavy.

Anthony ran lightly over the sand and the lines of seaweed brought in by the tide. He climbed over the wreck of the *Tempest,* a wooden boat that had washed ashore long before Anthony was born, and moved up over the rocks, where a few raspberry canes were bowed down with scarlet fruit. The berries reminded him of the hard candy he usually found in his Christmas stocking.

Growing weary, he climbed back up the cliff and returned to the woods. He almost burst with pride when he looked at the pail of glorious colors and smells. The sun was high—the time must have been almost noon—and Anthony was hot and thirsty. His flannel shirt stuck to him, his sneakers were wet, and the laces had come untied.

Then he stumbled into a woodchuck hole and fell hard. Anthony's heart thumped, and he could feel it pounding in his ears. But not one berry had spilled from the pail! On the ground where he had fallen, he saw a wild strawberry leaf and a handful of late stragglers calmly waiting for him to plop them into his pail. Which he did.

A chipmunk scolded him from the limb of a gnarled apple tree, and as Anthony looked up, two scabby green apples fell to his feet. Well, he thought as he picked them up, if they want to get into the jam, why not?

He had just about reached the kitchen door of his house when he saw one lonely stalk of rhubarb that had not yet gone to seed, so he picked it, topping off the mounded pail of fruit.

Anthony's neck had bumps from mosquito bites, and his arms were scratched from thorns that had torn through his sleeves. But all he felt was pride as he showed the bounty of fruit to his mother and told her what he wanted to do. She wiped her hands on her apron, looking quite pleased.

"What a great idea, Anthony. Let's do it!" She went down cellar and brought up some empty glass jars that had once held mustard and honey and candied cherries. While his mother washed them, Anthony got out the jam pot and the sugar and the wax. He pitted the cherries, stemmed the currants, hulled the berries, and cut up the apples and rhubarb. He picked some leaves and a tiny white spider out of the fruit. Then, in the pot, he crushed everything together with a potato masher, watching the colors run together.

Something was missing, he thought. Something yellowish. He looked in the refrigerator and found a small orange on its way to being dried up. He sliced it as thinly as he could without also slicing his finger, and added it to the mixture.

His mother lit the stove and put the pot on the burner. Anthony carefully added the sugar and began to stir. Soon the fruit started to boil and sputter up in thick bubbles that broke with a satisfying *blurp*. Every few minutes, they skimmed the foam from the bubbling surface with a big metal spoon. Finally, Anthony's mother tested the jam and declared it ready to pour. He stuck a knife inside each jar so it wouldn't crack when the hot fruit touched the glass. When the jars were almost full, Anthony carefully poured the hot, melted wax from the metal teapot and sealed each jar to the very top.

Then he spread some of the skimmings on a corn muffin and sat down with it on the back steps. He ate it with a slow, deep joy. Anthony's dream had come true. Never had he tasted anything so delicious!

When he went back into the kitchen to get another muffin, his mother asked, "Anthony, what will you call your jam?"

Anthony thought and thought. Then he took out a pencil and filled a sheet of paper with ideas—and many scratchings-out. Finally he said, "I've got it! I've got the just-right name," and he read out loud, very slowly:

STRAZZLECHERRYGOOSELCURRANTBLACKANDBLUEBARB JAM

"Oh, my," said his mother. "That will never fit on the label! How about just MAINE MARMALADE?"

Anthony wrote the new name on his scratch pad and considered it thoughtfully. Then he nodded his approval and continued to write, adding, "with two green apples."